MDLG Bedtime Stories

A collection of erotic lesbian age play short stories for ABDL and the Mommy Dommes who love them

By Tina Moore

Table of Contents

Claiming Taylor

I had seen her board the train in the morning and get off at her stop in the afternoon for months. Being a regular commuter was like that. We got to know who got on at what stop, who worked where or who only caught the train when their wife had taken the car to work. We even had a system of simple gestures to match. A faint knowing smile if your eyes happened to meet as you got off the train, the knowledge in the fact that you'd be seeing those same faces again tomorrow.

She had become a regular two months ago, but from the moment I first saw her, I wanted her. I knew what she wanted by the way she swayed her hips. I knew she needed me by the longing stare she gave the other businesswomen who stood with power and certainty. With her playful bounce down the platform as she saw the train approaching and her toothy smile when she looked out the window, it was not just me who noticed her. Businessmen would shift their briefcases in front of her crotches sooner than later when she stood next to them. The jolt and surge of the train making her sway against them as she found her footing was too much for them to bear.

"Here, take my seat," I heard her say to a mother of two small children. The train was unusually crowded today. It was near winter, and the weather made it cool one moment and warm the next. Looking at her outfit, it was clear she was trying to be dressed for both. Her baby pink fluffy sweater was pulled tightly over her large perky breasts and the white mini skirt which she wore to match complimented her slim legs. She got up, allowing the mother her seat and stumbled into a man who grabbed her arm, steadying her.

"Can't have you hurting your pretty little self," he said, making her pull away uncomfortably. She began to make her way down the aisle, pushing past men who refused to move, forcing her to rub against them to pass until she reached the end of the aisle. Her blonde pigtails flashed in the reflection of the window, and I looked up to see her standing beside my single seat, her purple backpack at her feet looking back up the aisle.

"I've seen you before, stop 439, right?" I ask her warmly. She looks at me, slight fear in her eyes, I wish it hadn't turned me on, seeing those big blue eyes go wide with caution.

"I get off on the last stop, so I kind of see everyone get on and off. I'm Sarah," I explain, holding out my hand. She looks down at my extended hand, and it occurs to me that this may be the most grown up thing she's done all day. Giggling she takes my hand and gently shakes it, smiling at me like she's just told me a secret.

"I'm Taylor. So how long have you been riding the train?" She asks. Before I can answer the train comes to a sudden stop making her stumble forward, falling onto me and clutching onto my shoulder for support. She blushes when she sees her hand in my lap and takes a moment before pulling away.

"This must be a new driver today or something," she says going even brighter. I just smile it had looked so sweet her 19-year-old hand with its painted pink nails on my business skirt covered thick thighs. I laugh kindly at her attempt to excuse her hand placement and answer her question.

The train reached Central station, and it filled with more people than I knew it would carry. I watched as three men pushed their way down the train to be close to Taylor, smiling as she had already agreed to give them blowjobs when they reached her.

"Hi there," one said, looking at her heavy tits clad in its fluffy cocoon. She ignored him, making him turn her around to face him.

"I said hi," he said. I don't think he was expecting me to stand up behind her and give him the warning look of his life. Taylor turned back towards me and bumped into me, not having realized I was so close. Before she could say a word, I took her hand, sat back down, and placed her firmly on my lap. She wiggled, trying to get away, but I stroked her hair and whispered that it was just so those men wouldn't harass her anymore.

"Wow thanks then," she said surprised someone would come to her rescue. We talked for the rest of the hour-long commute past the city and suburbs and into the edge of the country. I learned Taylor was studying the arts at the local university and that she wanted to become a painter. I told her about my big fancy job and felt my pussy get warm when she told me she thought it was cool. The train continued to rock, pushing her against my breasts, neatly packed away in the designer blazer I had recently purchased. I wrapped my arms around Taylor as she leaned into me and enjoyed the sensation of her resting her head on my shoulder.

"What about a boyfriend, do you have one?" I asked her letting my hand drop onto her lap, my fingers playing with the hem of her incredibly short skirt. Taylor shifted on my lap; I could have been sure she spread her legs wider as she settled in her new position.

"No, I haven't found anyone I would want to be with yet," she replied, slightly pushing her pussy out. I reached under her skirt and stroked her thigh, feeling the soft crease between her thigh and her panty line. Taylor looked at me in surprise, but I just smiled back at her and held her firmly on my lap by pressing my hand against her tummy.

"Um and what about you, do you have a boyfriend?" She asked, placing her hand over mine as I reached up and stroked her full breast over her fluffy sweater. It made her tits look even bigger than I knew they would be, exciting me as her nipple got hard when I pull it through the thick, soft material.

"No. I do not need a boyfriend," I replied. "I prefer having a baby girl like you," I added whispering in her ear all the while groping her fluffy tits. My other hand had been resting on the top of her pussy, and as she looked at me in shock by my response, I slipped a finger between her thighs, feeling her warmth and her wetness against her ruffled panties.

The people who had been around us had long gone, and there were only an older man and his wife three seats up as I pulled her panties to the slide and stroked along her slit making her squirm on my lap.

"Stay still for me baby girl, Mommy wants to feel you," I instructed looking Taylor in her wide eyes until she settled for me, I didn't want her bringing any attention to us. I reached under her sweater to discover she wasn't wearing a shirt, just a frilly bra which had ruffles at the front, no doubt matching her panties. I cupped one of her tits and squeezed, delighted at the feeling of her rocking on my lap in pleasure. Her nipple was hard, and I pinched it, making her gasp. I smiled and continued to grope her like the baby slut she was. Fingering and flicking her nipples predatorily with one hand while my other hand stroked her clit. I could feel she was close. It was hard to decide if I wanted her to cum in her panties or not, if I wanted to bring her to ecstasy and leave her sitting in her cummy panties or if I wanted to take her home with me and use her all night. I knew her stop was only one stop away as I pushed another finger along her slit. Pulling on her tits, I began whispering in her ear, "Who's Mommy's good little girl. Cum for Mommy baby, make your panties wet for me." I coaxed as cum spilled from her pussy, dripped from her slit and wet her panties as we passed her stop. I smile she was mine now. I didn't have to decide what I wanted to do with her. I was going to do everything.

Looking around nervously, Taylor realized she had missed her stop. She tried to get up, but I wrapped my bigger legs around hers, holding her in place as I slowly began to rub her again. I held her close to me by her tit and felt my panties moisten at her struggle.

"It's OK baby girl, get off with Mommy at the next stop, and I'll drive my sweet girl home," I told her, making her calm down again. I grabbed at her breast once more, pulling up her bra making her tits bounce a few times before I took my hand from under her sweater and stroked over the top, straightening it down for her and patting her like she was my pet. I wiped her cum on the front of her panties as I took my hand from under her skirt, pulling it up to see the mess she had made. Satisfied with myself, I patted her thigh to get up and held her steady getting up behind her, taking her backpack and my briefcase in one hand and her hand with my other and led her down the aisle to the train door.

"My house isn't far," I said, leading her off the platform into an alley. She was scared, I could tell, but this kind of scared wasn't sexy, so I stopped walking and pulled her into an embrace she eagerly accepted.

"It's OK. I walk down here all the time, and nothing bad has ever happened. I'll protect you little one, Mommy will keep you safe," I didn't want her to try and escape me. Taking her hand once more, we continued the walk to my house.

"You're right it wasn't far," Taylor said as I led her up the garden path to the back entrance of my home. Nestled between two large trees was the door to the garage, I was hoping I could convince her to stay a little longer than she currently had planned.

We walked in, and I clicked on the switch. It was my garage, but I had had it turned into a dungeon. I knew I liked it, but I was glad when I saw Taylor gingerly touching the fucking machine I had next to the king size bed. Hearing my heels on the concrete, she turned around quickly.

"I was just," Taylor tried to say before I pushed a pacifier gag into her mouth and groped her left breast. I kept my fingers on the gag, making sure she knew not to take it out. I took a step back and looked at her, my hands on my hips, her holding the gag in her mouth, her nipples pushing through her fluffy sweater.

"You were just what young lady? Thinking you could touch my things without permission?" I asked, stepping forward and buckling the gag behind her head. I pushed her back, making her fall on the bed. She was enveloped by the thick quilt and abundance of pillows, her small hands forcing them away as she tried to get up.

"No," I said sternly before turning away from her. I walked over to the glass cupboard and took out a pair of fluffy pink panties with a long slit from clit to arsehole, a white-tailed bunny butt plug and a tube of lube. I strolled over to where Taylor lay in the middle of the big bed, the navy linen making her outfit stand out even further.

"Take off your shoes for Mommy," I ordered placing the items down on the bed next to her. She quickly and obediently followed my command, putting her shoes neatly together on the floor.

"You have good manners little girl," I said, grabbing her by her tit and pulling her forward. I grabbed at her pussy, and she jumped, feeling her now cold but still wet cum push into her, and I laughed, making her blush.

"Give me these, I have something else you're going to wear," I instructed, holding out my hand and waiting. Taylor slowly pulled down her frilly panties and handed them to me. Putting them down next to her shoes, I took the panties I had for her and slowly pulled them up her thighs.

"I know you'll like the feel of this baby girl. Mommy has everything you'll like today," I whispered in her ear as I moved the fluffy panties over her arse, lightly scratching her as they were secured. I took the lube and butt plug, holding it up for her to see.

"Don't fight me on this or you'll get a spanking, and it'll still go in, do you understand?" I asked as I lube the medium sized plug. I knew it would stretch her; I had chosen it for that reason. I finished lubing it and watched as Taylor nodded in understanding as I climbed on top of her and began toying with her arsehole. I pushed my finger into her and then rubbed her clit with my other hand until I heard her moan, watching as she rolled her head back in pleasure and becoming startled as she felt my finger being replace with the tip of the plug.

"Don't be scared, Mommy is here," I coaxed as I pushed it into her, enjoying the slightest whimper as her arsehole was filled with more than it was ready to take. I pushed it in until there was nothing more than the cute little bunny tail showing and rolled her onto her tummy so I could see. Every movement now caused her to moan or gasp. I pushed her down on the bed and ran my hands up the backs of her thighs, stopping to grab and grope her arse cheeks, spreading them and pushing the plug into her.

"Mommy's good little princess," I said, rolling her back over.

"Keep that on," I commanded seeing her reach for her sweater wanting it off. I wanted her uncomfortable and horny. I wanted her to know that I was the source of her pleasure or pain. Walking over to the fucking machine I moved it, so its wide thick cock was pointing straight at Taylor's wet pussy.

"Where do you think this will go?" I teased, seeing her back up towards the head of the bed.

"And where do you think you are going?" I added, grabbing her by the wrist and quickly cuffing her right wrist to the bedpost.

"What did I say about fighting Mommy princess?" I asked, turning her onto her tummy and coming down hard and fast onto her arse, making her yelp in surprise and pain.

"I think I said not to do it," I added knowingly after spanking her again, this time harder than before. I rubbed her arse and gently turned her around to lay on her back, looking up at me.

"If it's too much let me know, OK?" I asked her seriously before smiling at her and kissing her forehead. She smiled behind the gag and nodded her head knowingly.

"But I've been watching you, the way you walk, the way you talk, the way you dress in these cute little clothes teasing people with your sluty pretend innocence. You were just waiting for a Mommy to take you home and make you her good girl, weren't you?" I asked, taking the lube and squirting it straight onto her clit. I opened the slit of the panties and rubbed the lube roughly between her lips before pulling the machine forward. Grabbing the cock which was about to be buried in her tight pussy, I rubbed the tip of it up and down her slit, pushing it slightly into her pussy. I stood up and push it over her, so that the lubed tip of the cock is above her pussy, dripping her cum and lube onto her panties. I tilt the machine down and pull her hips up, making her hold herself in position as I force the tip of the cock into her pussy, making her keep it in there.

"Ready baby girl?" I say as I turn on the machine. Taylor moans and her legs almost buckle as the cock filled her pussy. I switch it off when it is entirely in her cunt and walk over to my cupboard happy with the knowledge that Taylor is stuck on the fat cock inside of her. I take a pair of nipple clamps and walking back to her, turning the machine on and watch as it exits her pussy glistening in cum and lube. It pushes back in, making her arsehole quiver resulting in her bunny tail shaking.

"Mommy likes that sweetie," I say excitedly lifting her sweater. I reach under and pull down the front of her bra and pull her tits out. I pinch her nipple as the cock rams into her, making her moan and close her eyes. Opening a clamp, I secure it to her nipple, making her eyes pop open and a groan escape from behind her gag. I pinch her other nipple with the clamp and flick them a few times before aggressively groping her swelling tits through her sweater. I slap her tits every time the cock reaches her hilt making her hips grind rhythmically in time.

"That's it, baby," I encourage, turning the machine up watching as cum oozes out around the thick cock fucking her. Standing up, I go to my high backed armchair and sit down, watching my pretty baby be fucked, forced to cum over and over, her legs shaking more intensely with each new orgasm. I smile as I watch her cum dripping onto the sheets, making a wet patch under her arse. Knowing she cannot take much more, I go back to her bed and come up behind her. I lift her under her armpits and move her onto my lap once more. She all but collapses into my arms and I reach down to rub her clit as another orgasm washes over her. I grab at her breasts, pulling on the nipple clamps until she yelps, causing my clit to throb.

"Last one baby," I loving say kissing her cheek as I turn the machine on faster, praising myself for buying the model which came with a remote. The cock fucks her forcefully, easily sliding in and out of her used cunt before she yells out and her legs give way. The cock comes flying out of her pussy and covers her fluffy panties and sweater in cum as it continues pumping forward and back over the top of her. I let it; I want her dirty. As she begins to breathe normally once more, I turn it off and push her hips down into her mess. Her legs are still shaking, and her face is flushed. I uncuff her wrists and take her hands, letting them flop down onto her tits as I place my hands over the top of hers, making her grope herself.

"Did Mommy make you cum too hard pretty baby?" I tease knowing the answer. Taylor just nods her head as she is forced to keep grabbing and squeezing her tits. She closes her eyes and rolls her head towards me, and I can see her pussy still leaking cum onto her thighs. I take my hands off hers and reach under unclamping the nipple clamps. Checking the clock, I see it's 8:30. *Time flies*, I think to myself as I gently unbuckle the pacifier gag. I reach for the panties and Taylor tries to lift her bottom for me, but her legs buckle and give way underneath her making me laugh.

"It's OK little one, Mommy's got it," I say, pulling them down off her. I took the butt plug out next and lay everything on the bed as I pull Taylor over to me and hold her in my arms.

"Did you want to go home now?" I asked stroking her check. She looks up at me and nervously touches my breasts over my blazer. I unbutton it as well as my red satin blouse and let her feel me.

"I am home," Taylor replies vulnerably making me smile knowing that I've claimed my baby girl at last.

Playing Doctors and Nurses

"There you are baby," Amanda said excitedly seeing Mindy walk into the bar. It was the monthly Kinksters mingle at a bar one of the members owned. This was Mindy's favorite night of the month when she could crawl around in the specially set up nursery at the far end of the bar and have her Mommy give her all her love. Amanda flung her arms around Mindy and took her hand immediately leading her to the area the owner had set up for the babies.

"No, you can't have that my love," Amanda told Mindy who reached for her wine. Amanda had worn Mindy's favorite outfit. A long white dress with brown knee-high boots and her hair done up in a messy bun. Mindy loved seeing Amanda, outside of these nights, she knew nothing about her. Not where she worked or what she did for fun other than treat Mindy like the most precious baby girl.

Amanda pushed Mindy gently to the padded floor and began to change her out of her adult clothes into something more appropriate for the evening. Mindy used to bring her clothes, diapers, and toys, but from the time she and Amanda had begun their relationship, Amanda had chosen what she would wear. Tonight she had chosen a yellow t-shirt with a white duck on the front and matching frilly socks. She didn't want a diaper cover on

Mindy tonight and left her duck print diaper exposed for everyone to see.

"Who's Mommy's pretty little princess," Amanda cooed as she shook a pacifier in Mindy's face waiting for her to part her lips.

"I am Mommy," Mindy excitedly replied, opening her mouth so Amanda could put the pacifier in. Amanda and Mindy played all night. A few times, other Mommy's came over to talk to Amanda and to compliment her on having such a well behaved baby. There were a few brats there on this particular evening, and Amanda was happy Mindy was not one of them.

"She's a good girl," Amanda said affectionately to another Mommy who was spanking her baby for not sharing the toys with the others while looking at Mindy who was making a tower out of the blocks.

As the night progressed and the Mommy's and Daddy's enjoyed more drinking, Mindy watched as one by one the other baby's found themselves bent over a knee or table taking a spanking.

"I'm a good girl, Mommy?" Mindy asked fearfully. She hoped it wouldn't be her next who would be spanked in front of the others.

"The very best, but if Mommy wants that little bottom of yours spanked red, that's what's going to happen, little girl," Amanda replied reading Mindy face and understanding her meaning. Luckily for Mindy, Amanda had chosen not to spank her that evening. She had felt Amanda's spankings before and knew they were not something taken lightly.

The night passed more quickly than Amanda or Mindy would have liked, and after what felt like far too soon Amanda was taking off Mindy's socks, diaper, and t-shirt and helping her get dressed in her grown-up clothes.

"I hate this part," Mindy said as she zipped up her jeans. Amanda smiled sympathetically and pulled her in for a hug.

"I know baby," she whispered patting Mindy's bottom.

Mindy woke up on the day she had been dreaming about. Today she would begin her first day at a newly built hospital as a Doctor for Oncology. She dressed in a cream-colored knee length pencil skirt with a light blue button-down blouse tucked in. Her shoes were a sensible height, a cream color which slipped perfectly over her nude pantyhose.

"Wow," Mindy said out loud as she let her thick wavy mane of light brown hair out and swayed, loosening the waves. Mindy was inducted and filed the required paperwork before she began to be introduced to the nurses who were on her ward. By lunch, her mind was spinning, and as she began to set up her office, she heard a knock at her door. Opening the door, she dropped the pen she was holding upon seeing Amanda stand opposite her on the other side of the door.

"I thought I taught you better than that," Amanda said in a

low tone pushing Mindy to the side and walking into her office. Mindy shut the door behind her and turned around to see Amanda sitting on the edge of her desk.

"Nice," she said, looking around admiring Mindy's taste.

"What are you doing here?" Mindy finally said in a hoarse voice. Amanda got up and walked to her, grabbing her by the hair and pulling it back as she had done when Mindy had been naughty at a previous meeting. It felt different her doing it now when it was just the two of them in this very adult setting.

"I work here and if you think I'm going to be taking any orders from you little girl you are sadly mistaken," Amanda replied, letting Mindy's hair go.

"I was never going to order you around, Mo, I mean Amanda. I just want to do my job," Mindy answered, a little whine escaping her voice and making Amanda smile victoriously.

"Do you think you're a big girl now in your pretty office and big girl clothes," Amanda teased pulling at Mindy's blouse from her skirt. Mindy quickly rushed to tuck it back in as Amanda pulled her into her and held her firmly. She began rubbing her arse over her skirt the way Mindy loved until she stopped struggling to break free.

"Mommy is going to come in here after work baby, and you are going to change into something a little bit more to my liking," Amanda said as she kissed Mindy's cheek and left the office.

Mindy waited for Amanda to arrive, but at 7 pm she decided to go home. Just as she was opening the door to her office, Amanda turned around the corner and began walking along the corridor to Mindy.

"I hope you weren't thinking of leaving when I told you to wait for me," Amanda said as she walked past Mindy and put her bag on Mindy's desk.

"Are you going to shut the door, or do you want everyone to see you, baby?" Amanda asked loudly, making Mindy shut the door quickly hoping no one heard her. Amanda laughed and began unpacking a diaper to Mindy's horror.

"I can't do that here, Amanda," Mindy hissed. Amanda walked over to Mindy, spun her around and spanked her hard on her arse.

"You'll call me Mommy here, there, every fucking where baby girl," Amanda said as she took a changing mat and powder in one hand and a diaper and pacifier in another.

"Lay down for Mommy," Amanda said as she placed the changing mat in the middle of the floor and patted it lovingly. Mindy approached slowly, and Amanda reached up and pulled her by the hand to the ground, making her whimper as she lay down. Amanda ran her hands up Mindy's skirt and pulled down her pantyhose until they were at her ankles. She took a pair of scissors and cut off Mindy's g-string and threw the ruined garment in the bin.

"You won't be needing this again," Amanda stated. Next, she made Mindy lift her bottom, and she slid the diaper underneath her. Amanda took out a double padded wad and made the diaper ever thicker between Mindy's legs making her begin to fuss.

"Now now baby girl Mommy knows what you need," Amanda said as she pushed a pink pacifier into Mindy's mouth and snapped her fingers at her angrily as she tried to take it out. Submitting, Mindy kept it in and began sucking on it as she fought not to enter her baby headspace. Amanda put fresh powder on Mindy and fastened the diaper in place, pushing it into Mindy who squirmed. She then took the pantyhose and rolled them back up Mindy's legs, pulling them over her puffy diaper, securing it in place. Amanda rolled down Mindy's skirt and enjoyed watching her fight herself as a big thick puffy diaper was locked in place over her grown-up skirt.

"That's more like it baby," Amanda said, looking at Mindy who still had a pink pacifier in her mouth.

"I know just the person who would like to see this," Amanda said as a knock came from the door. Mindy's eyes went wide, and she tried to stop Amanda, who only grabbed her by the hair and pulled her back. As Amanda opened the door, Mindy was stunned to see the director of the hospital standing there looking at her. The director was in her mid 50', and her mean stare and womanly body made Mindy excited and nervous at the same time.

"You said you had a good girl, but I hadn't realized she would be so easily babied," the director exclaimed locking the door behind her.

"You can call me Auntie Lisa baby Mindy. I'm going to have some fun with you," the director said slowly unbuttoning Mindy's blouse. Mindy looked from Amanda to the director and was lost as to what to do. Before she knew it her blouse was on the floor and so was her skirt and heels. The director had tied her wrists behind her back and was pulling up a frilly pink skirt over Mindy's large diaper. Even with the pantyhose squishing it down, Mindy's diaper exaggeratedly stuck out from the rest of her. The director sat on the floor, and Amanda pushed Mindy down, making her fall on her face and letting out a whimper of pain.

"Oh, did the baby hurt herself?" The director cooed picking Mindy up and laying her upwards across her lap. Mindy slowly nodded her head, feeling herself seep into her little headspace. Amanda noticed it too and came over with Mindy's favorite blankie snuggling it into her face. Before Mindy realized she had the director's womanly breast in her mouth and was being rocked as she nursed.

"She likes that," Amanda said, looking at Mindy's fluttering eyes.

"She'll be asleep soon, and milk will spill from her pretty mouth, here," Amanda added, handing the director an extra cloth to mop up Mindy.

"That promotion you put in for. You just got it," the director said to Amanda, who kissed Mindy's head.

"Thank you," she replied, walking to the door, leaving Mindy in the arms of the director and her mouth full of her milk. *Amanda was right; she is a sleeping girl*, the director thought as she felt Mindy's body become heavy with sleep. The director had already planned for Mindy to start a week later her coming in today was solely for this. The director dressed again and knowing the ways out of the hospital, which would cause the least attention, she picked up Mindy and carried her to her car. When Mindy was all buckled in, the director turned the car on and began the drive to her house.

"Where am I?" Mindy asked as she sleepily woke up from the bumps on the road. The director put her hand on the front of Mindy's diaper and rubbed it lovingly.

"You're alright, baby girl. Your Mommy and I have decided I will look after you for one week and she will look after you every other week. We know how much you love being cared for, and now you can be cared for more than a few hours a month," the director explained pushing on Mindy's bladder making her squirm. Mindy hadn't realized Amanda would take her complaint about leaving the bar quite so far.

"But I have to work; you hired me!" Mindy said as she continued to squirm under the director's touch.

"You'll be starting next week baby girl. Then you'll be changed and fed and come home with me for a week, and the following week you'll do whatever your Mommy wants you to do. Don't bother complaining about it; the decision has already been made," the director sternly replied pinching Mindy's nipples over the pink long sleeve she had dressed her in while she was asleep.

"Here we are baby," she said, pulling into a dark garage and closing the door before getting out. The director came around to Mindy's side and let her out, taking her hand and leading her inside. Mindy's diaper was so thick she had to waddle, and the director loved seeing her new little girl have to waddle fast to keep up. The director brought Mindy to a room which made her gasp. She saw a cot and a changing table, a locked fully enclosed cage which had a padded floor and stuffed toys, a toy box and a rocking horse which had a pair of hand and ankle cuffs attached to it.

"Do you like it, little girl?" The director asked as Mindy dropped to her knees and crawled into the room. She began looking through the toy box and found a big soft yellow duck she dragged around the floor with her by the wing. The director smiled as she watched Mindy touch the cage nervously.

"That's where naughty babies go. You're not a naughty

baby, are you sweetie?" The director asked coming over and opening the cage door, laughing when Mindy quickly crawled to the other side of the room and shook her head. The director pulled Mindy to her feet and led her to the rocking horse.

"You're going to play here while I sort out some dinner alright baby," she explained as she cuffed Mindy's wrists and ankles to the horse and used the remote to make it start rocking. Mindy was surprised it had come with a remote. She was also surprised at how narrow the place to sit was. As the rocking horse moved forward and back, Mindy could feel the thin piece of wood between her legs push into her diaper and rub her pussy. Before long, the motion of back and forth has separated Mindy's pussy lips, and her clit was being forcefully rubbed along the diaper as she rocked. The director came back into the room and watched as Mindy was made to cum by the rocking horse and smiled, seeing her nipples go hard and her hips grind down into her diaper.

"It looks like someone is enjoying themselves," the director said as she watched Mindy cum for the fifth consecutive time.

"It feels so good Auntie Lisa," Mindy replied, making the directors own clit begin to tingle.

"Come on; you've had enough now. We are going to eat dinner," the director instructed, turning the rocking horse off and uncuffing Mindy. She helped Mindy down and patted her diapered bottom a few times as she led Mindy into the living room.

Mindy was placed in an adult-sized highchair and fed dinner, then taken to the bathtub and washed before the director changed her diaper and put her in pajamas.

"You are just the sweetest," the director said fastening Mindy's purple mittens with a lock on her wrists. Mindy had never worn these before, and they felt strange. She shook her hands, seeing if they would come off, but they didn't.

"Baby, do you think I'd make them loose enough for you to get them off?" The director laughed, seeing Mindy's attempt. She put Mindy in the cot and locked her mittens to a chain which was connected to the cot.

"You're not going to go anywhere little girl. You're mine for a week, and I plan to keep it that way," the director said as she tugged on the chains making sure they were securely in place. The director turned off the lights and shut the door as Mindy clapped her hands as she saw the glow in the dark stars that covered the ceiling.

The weeks passed, just like the director had said. For the week Mindy was the director's baby, and for every other week, she was Amanda's. During the day she was the new Doctor with an impressive office and had many a male nurse flirt with her, and by night she was diaper-clad and breastfed. It wasn't the life

Mindy had thought she would have for herself; it was better.

Moonlight Circus

Mia loved the circus. Ever since she had been taken by her mother when she was six years old, she knew the circus is where she wanted to be. Fast forward twenty years and after a lifetime of gymnastics and strict dieting, she was ready.

Mia had seen them advertising with their signature marketing style, a series of chalk graffiti around the city with their emblem. She had jumped at the chance and had taken a taxi to their performing tents in the showgrounds. Captivated by the dark blue and silver stripes of the big top, Mia nervously had approached a woman sweeping the entrance.

"Hi, I'm looking for Madam, I'm here about your advertisement," Mia said, hoping the woman would be helpful.

"Oh really, what do you do?" The woman asked, placing her broom to the side and smiling at Mai.

"I'm an acrobat," Mia replied, feeling silly as she had said it with such enthusiasm. The woman giggled and gestured for Mia to follow her into the tent.

As they passed through the tent, Mia tried not to look star struck as she saw other people performing. There were body contortionists and other acrobats performing at heights Mia had never attempted; she hoped she wouldn't have to audition with them watching.

"Madam," the woman politely called as she knocked on a

red wooden door.

"Enter my darling," came a flamboyant voice from inside. The woman turned the intricate brass handle and held the door open for Mia, who took the hint and walked inside. Closing the door behind her, Mia turned around to see the woman had gone.

"So you have come about the job," Madam stated more than asked. Mia took in her form. She had been some sort of dancer in her youth. She moved with an elegance and grace Mia had not seen before, her slender body almost snaking its way around her as Madam circled Mia.

"An acrobat," Madam said, stepping back and looking at Mia.

"Yes. How did you know?" Mia said excitedly. Madam shook her head and put her finger to her lips.

"I ask the questions. You, my little acrobat merely answer them," Madam replied. Mia nodded and moved from one foot to another.

"You may show me now," Madam instructed expectantly. Mia snapped into life and remembered why she was here in the first place. *She's mesmerizing;* Mia thought as Madam led her to the performing floor.

Mia auditioned as though her life depended on it. She wanted this job yet she felt a strange feeling of not wanting to disappoint Madam, a woman how had hardly spoken to her whom she had met a mere ten minutes earlier. As Mia performed, she felt

Madam's eyes on her the whole time, taking in her form, her positioning, the way she landed and her connection to the audience who had stopped what they were doing and come over to watch her.

"She's perfect," Madam stated, turning off the music.

"You may stop," she added as Mia turned to see why the music had stopped. Mia slowly made her way back to the group who waited for her below. She had thought it was strange that Madam was the only one out of the six people she counted who was standing. The others were sitting at her feet, one woman even cuddling her leg as she leaned against her.

"Bravo Mia," Madam stated as she clapped purposefully. Mia blushed and looked around the tent, relieved to see the others smiling at her.

"Thank you; I hope you liked it," Mia replied.

"I liked it very much. Enough to offer you the opening position, you will start tomorrow night." Madam instructed.
Mia practically skipped home. I impressed Madam! She thought to herself. And I also got my dream job? She said, questioning herself as to why she was more relieved that she had proven herself to Madam than get the job she had worked so hard to become a professional in.

Mia woke up early the next day, still in a haze from the previous day. She got ready and felt like she was floating on air as she entered the big top. Madam had told her to come and see her first thing when she arrived.

"Good morning my sweet one," Madam gushed, seeing Mia. She embraced her, and Mia had to force herself not to melt into Madam's arms as she was held longer than Mia usually hugged a person. Breaking the embrace Madam took Mia's hand and showed her where she would change and told her that rehearsal was in 30minutes.

"I hope you are ready; I want nothing, but you're absolute best. Think yesterday but better," Madam instructed as she left Mia to change.

Coming out into rehearsal, Mia was greeted by the other performers. She spun, flipped and twirled until she thought her body could take no more, and that's when Madam told her to do it all again. She made them do full performance rehearsals back to back for 5 hours, and at 4 pm she finally called out stop.

"Very good, come here," she instructed the group of 6 acrobats who formed a line one behind another. Mia was confused as to want was going on, but she joined the queue, annoyed she was pushed to the back.

"No, let my new baby come to the front," Madam ordered making Mia confused. The other acrobats turned to face her, the one who had been first in line smiling encouragingly. Mia slowly walked towards Madam, who had her arms wide open. Her chestnut hair flowed over her firm breasts, and Mia swallowed hard when she caught herself looking wantonly at them.

"Tonight is Mia's first performance. If anything is going to go wrong it will be tonight, and I need all of you to make it look like it was meant to happen," Madam said as she rubbed Mia's back. The others just stood there nodding in agreement and where dismissed.

"Mia," Madam called when Mia was almost about to exit the tent. She turned around and saw Madam gesturing for her to come over to her. Reluctantly, Mia began to walk to Madam, who silently took her hand.

"I want to make sure your muscles will not be too sore tonight. Come," Madam ordered. Mia was taken to Madam's caravan and instructed to lie down on her bed.

"Take them off," Madam said nodding to Mia's training tights. Slowly Mia rolled them down, but she was too slow for Madam who began to pull them down to her ankles to hurry her up. Madam reached for Mia's panties, and Mia resisted, trying to push Madam's hands away.

"Shh silly girl," Madam cooed. She took Mia in her arms and managed to have Mia bare arsed within a moment.

"There," Madam stated in satisfaction.

"What are you doing?" Mia said softly. Madam looked at her and frowned.

"I thought I told you I would be the one asking the questions," she replied.

"You cannot break my rules. I'm hurt you do not trust me. Have I not been lovely to you?" Madam asked.

"Yeah you have but, this?" Mia questioned. Madam stood up and grabbed Mia's arm, pulling her onto her lap and spanking her arse before Mia knew what was happening.

"Stop fussing little girl; you will learn to trust Mommy. Take your punishment like a good girl," Madam ordered sternly spanking her arse again. Madam covered Mia's mouth and continued to beat her until her arse was red and blotchy. Each time her strike feeling more intense than the last Mia stopped fighting and lay limb over Madam's lap. When she was finished, Madam stood Mia up.

"There are three hours before we open, try to be a good girl until then," Madam instructed, passing Mia her panties and tights and leaving her to get changed.

Mia didn't remember how her first performance went, her mind was still on the spanking, how Madam referred to herself as Mommy, and how everyone seemed to know Mia had been spanked. *Had they heard? Does this happen a lot?* Mia asked herself as she was given the fourth sympathetic look in a row. One of the other acrobats had even left a bottle of lotion on top of her bag with a note saying she might find this useful.

As the last of the tidying up was done, Mia found herself alone. She had been told by Madam to stay after the show, even though

Mia wasn't living with them yet she still needed to be a part of the end of show celebrations. She walked around the tent wondering where everyone was as she hears Madam call for her. Mia made her way to the room where she had received her first spanking and froze when she arrived.

"Come in baby," Madam said. She was surrounded by the other performers, all 9 of them. Some were drawing, some were watching a movie and eating popcorn, and some were reading. What they all had in common was they were in diapers and wearing baby clothes. The pictures they were drawing were with crayons, the movie they were watching was something Mia watched when she was younger, and the books they were reading were picture books. Madam smiled as she saw Mia take it all in.

"Well, baby, are you going to come to Mommy or not?" Madam asked, patting her lap. Mia looked around the room again and felt herself move towards Madam. She opened her arms and sat Mia on her lap, giving her a blankie to hold onto.

"You may call me Madam by day sweet darling, but after the show my name is Mommy. If you choose to stay with us, you will be my littlest baby, and I will love you so. Your brothers and sisters will play gently with you, and Mommy will make sure nothing bad happens to you. Would you like that my little one?" Madam asked in a friendly tone that made Mia finally melt into her arms. Knowingly, Madam took a pacifier and wiggled it between Mia's lips, making her giggle.

"I thought so," Madam stated in satisfaction. She stood up and took Mia to an empty corner of her caravan and snapped her fingers to the floor.

"Down baby," Madam instructed watching as Mia sat down. Madam took a diaper and a white shirt, pink terry toweling dungarees and matching socks. She pushed Mia to the floor and smiled at how compliant she was.

"Mommy's going to change you every night sweetheart, once the show is over, you're my sweet baby girl in her sweet baby clothes again," Madam stated while peeling Mia's clothes off. Powdering her for the first time made Mia sneeze and the woman who Mia had met on the first day, Tiffany, waddled over to where she was laying,

"The movie is finished Mommy," Tiffany said, sitting down next to Madam who was now rubbing her hands over Mia's diaper-clad pussy.

"Alright, honey. You need to let Mommy finish dressing baby Mia first, and then I'll put on another one. Have you and Sammy decided what you want next?" Madam asked to see Tiffany shaking her head. Madam kissed the top of Tiffany's head and patted her bottom as she crawled back to where the TV was. Madam then took the white shirt and wriggled it over Mia's head, followed by the dungarees. Finishing it off with her socks, Mia was surprised when Madam effortlessly picked her up and carried her through the caravan. She held Mia on her hip while she put on another movie and sat on the long black couch and bounced Mia on her lap.

Madam decided she wanted a tea and getting up she had put Mia down on the floor to play with Tiffany and Sammy. Sammy had played puppets with her making her giggle and clap her hands excitedly, and Tiffany had shown her the sticker book Madam had bought her the previous week. As Mia became sleepy, she crawled over to Madam who was reading with one of her other babies and Mia reached out for her.

"Oh, is someone tired?" Madam asked knowingly. She had put Mia through the rigorous rehearsal before the show deliberately she had been waiting for this. Mia nodded and sleepily rubbed her eyes.

"Yes, Mommy," Mia replied as she climbed onto Madam's lap to hear the end of the story. When the story was over, Madam instructed that she would be back shortly and that when she came back, everyone was going to sleep. She didn't wait to hear the reply as she lifted Mia onto her hip again and carried her into the bedroom.

"You will sleep with me every night little girl," Madam stated, pulling back the sheets. She gently placed Mia down, who nodded in agreement. As she settled into Madam's big bed, she touched her diaper, making Madam laugh.

"That stays on baby girl," she explained. Madam pushed

Mia's hands away as she rubbed the diaper through her fuzzy dungarees.

"Why do you think I keep you in them, baby because you'll wet yourself if I let you take it off. Baby girls can't have big girl panties," Madam cooed. Mia pouted and looked away.

"That's right baby girl; Mommy fully expects you to have a full wet diaper in the morning. You don't want to make Mommy cross again, do you? Let's have a practice now; I have a sneaky feeling you need to wet your diaper. Come on, sweetheart; Mommy will change you after," Madam coaxed feeling Mia through her dungarees and diaper, feeling for them to become warm and full. Mia tried to refuse, but Madam pointed to the cane on her bookshelf.

"Trust Mommy when I say you don't want to feel that on your pretty little bottom sweetheart," Madam said making Mia instantly wet her diaper. She began to cry, and Madam smiled, enjoying the power she had over her. Madam began to sing to Mia, soothing her with soft, heartfelt rhythm as she changed her.

"Mommy's clean baby," Madam stated patting Mia's new fresh diaper. Madam had made this one unusually thick, forcing Mia's thighs to remain open, exposing her diaper-clad pussy. Madam rubbed her and sung her to sleep, turning the light off and shutting the door quietly behind her.

Mia woke the next morning before anyone else. She lay next to Madam who had dressed in just a singlet and shorts and snuggled into her smiling when Madam pulled her in and held her tight.

"Good morning, little girl," Madam suddenly said, making Mia happy she was still Madam's baby.

"Good morning, Mommy," Mia replied. Madam opened her eyes and smiled at Mia.

"The sun is up, my darling. Once that diaper is off, and you are in your big girl clothes, don't get caught calling me Mommy, understand?" Madam stated lovingly, but there was a warning in her voice nonetheless.

"OK, Mommy," Mia replied, sad it would be over shortly. As if reading her mind, Madam reached down and rubbed her pussy tenderly.

"Don't worry baby; it's only for a little while. Every night you'll be Mommy's special little girl. But both shows must go on," Madam explained reassuringly.

Madam continued to rub Mia's pussy and began to make her grind herself down on her hand as Madam cleared her throat and raised an eyebrow expectantly. Mia gave her a puzzling look before remembering she needed to wet her diaper. She was relieved Madam didn't spank her again for forgetting as she filled her diaper making Madam smile and close her eyes as she fell back asleep leaving Mia to lay in her wet diaper for another hour.

As the months went on, Mia became accustomed to her daily routine of training and performing and nightlife as Madam's baby. Enjoying the freedoms of the adult world during the day, and happily let Madam treat her as a baby by night. Madam had a way of making her feel like she was the most special of them all, but Mia was careful not to show it, she was pretty sure the others felt the same way she did. Madam had that way about her. She could walk into a room of one hundred people and have each of them leaving with the feel of being the only one in the room. When a newspaper journalist asked her why the Moonlight Circus was the most famous Circus in modern history, she just laughed and said, "We are a family." She had read that out to everyone over breakfast, making half of them laugh, and the other half choke on their food.

"A family, how very poetic," Tiffany said as she buttered her toast.

"Yes a family, with you Madam at the head of this very close family," Sammy added, making even Madam laugh.

"Well I had to make it somewhat entertaining, she was incredibly dreary," Madam said defensively smiling at Mia. Mia smiled back but looked down at her breakfast.

"What is it, Mia?" Madam asked sensing something was wrong.

"Nothing," Mia lied, making the table silent. Madam walked to where she was sitting and bent down to meet her eyes.

"Mia," Madam said warningly. Mia looked around and felt her face begin to blush. She pulled up her skirt, and Madam saw her diaper was still on.

"Yes, because that's what babies need Mia," Madam explained. Mia looked at her inquisitively, unsure of how to form her question without making it a question. Sammy looked down and suppressed his laugh; he had learned the hard way not to laugh at his adult baby brothers and sisters.

"Oh Mia, come on then," Madam finally said, seeing Mia's embarrassment. She stood up and took Mia by the hand, lifting Mia's skirt to show the table the front of her diaper.

"The baby doesn't want to be Mommy's baby any longer," Madam stated. Mia pulled away, but Madam's grip was firm.

"Maybe I wanted you to be my baby a little bit longer today, Mia? Hey, did you think about that? Now that the tour is over, maybe I wanted you in diapers during the day as well," Madam explained as she rubbed the front of Mia's diaper in front of everyone making her blush red. Tiffany stood up and came to stand next to Madam.

"Can I be in diapers during the day as well please Madam?" Tiffany asked. Madam took a step back in shock.

"You must want this pretty bad if you are willing to be spanked just for asking," Madam said as Tiffany nodded yes.

"Very well we have three weeks until we move to another

city and begin the next tour. If you are in my caravan by the time that door shuts, you can be my baby until we move out," Madam said laughing as she picked up Mia and watched as the others ran to her caravan door.

Comic store Mommy

Jessie had been coming to the comic store around the corner from her apartment ever since she and James moved into the neighbor. James had thought it was silly, Jessie had never even read a comic let alone owned a collection of them. He would tease her when she went out to the weekly comic book club meeting stating that he couldn't believe she would rather spend her evening with a bunch of loser virgin nerds than spend time with him. Jessie would stay silent during his taunts, knowing that staying in and spending the night with him would mean laying on her stomach as he took her from behind. Pounding her pussy with his chubby cock and full, hairy balls with monotonous repetition until he cream pied her hole and began in her arse until that too was dripping with his cum. She never came. How could she when he thought foreplay was titty fucking her and finishing in her mouth? When she had tried to show him ways to gently touch her clit or to lick her pussy, but he hadn't been interested, continuing to use her as his cum whore. The comic book club was her night off from being fed his cock and pumped full of his cream. Her night where Sally would make choc chip cookies and hot tea, where the people would be interested in what she had to say and make her feel like she belonged to something meaningful.

She wanted to leave home early, telling James the group had something important to discuss.

"Well, you know what's waiting for you when you get home," he started pulling out his already hard cock, lifting her skirt and rubbing it up and down her panty clad arse crack.

"James!" Jessie exclaimed, pulling away and grabbing her bag. As she bent over, she felt him again at her arse, hands groping under her skirt, pulling her arse cheeks apart and pressing his fingers to push her lips open. *Great,* Jessie thought in discontent feeling him tap his cock against her panties. He lifted the side of her panties and placed his cock underneath. Jessie felt the wet pre-cum rub against her arse cheek as he grabbed her by the hips and rubbed his cock on her bare skin.

"James, I have to go," Jessie said, pushing his hands off her hips.

"Shh," James replied, wrapping an arm around her waist, using his body weight to bend her over and stuck his thumb in her mouth. Jessie tried to use her tongue to push his big thumb out of her mouth, but it was held in place by his hand, which was firmly squeezing her face. He eventually took it out of her mouth and reached under her skirt once more, taking his cock out from under her panties and pulling them down in one quick motion. Still bending her over and holding her again with his other hand, he guided his cock into her pussy and stuck his thumb up her arse.

"You're not going until those panties are wet with my cum. I want those fucking nerds to know you're mine." He stated aggressively as he pounded her from behind. Jessie stopped struggling; she knew she would be late, but what could she do? James had her bent over, her pussy full of his cock and his thumb in her arse. He took his hand from her waist and grabbed her arm and pushed her against the front door. Jessie knew he was close; she could feel him cumming inside of her. As he reached his climax, he pulled out and held his cock over her panties, covering them in his load. Some of his copious thick white cream fell onto the floor but most filled Jessie's panties. Jessie felt his thumb pull out of her arse and jumped when she felt him pull her panties up. His hand cupping her from the front and from behind. He rubbed her cum loaded panties firmly on her pussy, pushing them into her cunt and arse. Jessie could feel his cum drip down her thighs. She was going to be late now, her bus would have already be gone from the bus stop, and another one would be another ten minutes. James wiped his cock on her arse cheek, wetting the outside of her panties.

"Have fun tonight," he said as he pushed her out of the house and quickly shut the door behind her. Jessie didn't have a key, James had said she didn't need one because he worked from home and would always be there when she finished work. She knocked on the door wanting to change her panties, but no answer came. She stood there, thinking about the choc chip cookies, warm tea, and people who made her feel valued, but she mostly thought about Sally. Sally, with her sweet smile and friendly manner, the way she would gently play with Jessie's hair every time she greeted her. Deciding she didn't want to miss out on that she headed towards the bus stop.

"Oh, I was beginning to think you couldn't make it!" Sally exclaimed, jumping up from the circle and rushing to greet Jessie at the door. Jessie smiled. Sally was wearing her favorite dress, the green and white poke-a-dot one that showed her ample cleavage. Sally's green eyes complimented the dress, and her long red hair made her look like a vision.

"Yeah sorry, I missed my bus," Jessie replied, not exactly lying. Sally took Jessie's hand and led her to the group, grabbing a cookie and pushing it into Jessie's mouth before turning back to lead her to the circle. Jessie giggled as she took the cookie from her lips and bit down happy they were still warm. She found her seat and shifted uncomfortably as James's cum squelched into her tender holes. Sally gave her a questioning look making her blush, and she quickly looked away, hoping to curb her curiosity.

The meeting ran like clockwork; she shared her thoughts about the recent comic book they were reviewing, the character development and the storyline. All the while aware Sally had hardly taken her eyes off her. As the meeting ended, Jessie waited until she was the last one still sitting in the circle. She didn't want to run the risk of someone seeing the wet patch on the back of her skirt she could feel most definitely there. She got up as Sally walked someone to the door, grabbing her bag and trying to push it behind her to cover her skirt.

"What are you doing?" Sally asked startling Jessie; she hadn't realized that Sally had been watching her from the door.

"Getting ready to go home?" Jessie replied, unsure of what the correct answer was. Sally locked the door and walked over to Jessie; she looked down at the bag she was pushing behind her and looked back up into Jessie's eyes.

"Have you had an accident?" Sally asked, wondering what Jessie was doing. Sally had seen Jessie's panties under her skirt during the meeting, as she was sitting directly opposite her and had noticed the evident change in color, indicating that she was wetter in some places than others.

"What no!" Jessie exclaimed taken aback. Sally thought for a moment before grabbing Jessie's bag, making her gasp in shock and blush in shame. Sally reached around to Jessie's bottom and gently patted her over her skirt.

"Well, whatever it is, I can't let you leave like that. Let's get you cleaned up," she stated, taking Jessie's hand and leading her out the back. Jessie knew James would be waiting for her. She knew that she was due home in 15 minutes. She was hoping whatever Sally had planned it wouldn't take too long.

Sally opened the office door and put Jessie's bag on the couch before leading her through another door. The room was dark, and Jessie held Sally's hand tighter nervous about being surrounded by blackness.

"It's OK Jessie, Sally is here, I'm going to take care of you," Sally said in her warm southern voice. Jessie felt Sally push her down onto something soft and lay next to her. She felt Sally hold her in a way that James never had and she sighed contently albeit involuntarily when Sally began to stroke her forehead.

"I thought you might need some loving little one, I hadn't realized you needed it so bad," Sally said, getting up. Jessie quickly felt for her, grabbing her arm and pulling her back down.

"It's OK; I'm just going to get you something. You'll be alright here for a moment," Sally explained reassuring. Sally waited until Jessie let go and got up. When Sally came back, she kissed Jessie's cheeks before reaching under her skirt and pulling her panties down.

"I'm just going to wipe you, clean baby," Sally stated, wiping a wet wipe over Jessie's pussy before cleaning her thighs, arsehole, and bottom.

"What happened baby girl?" Sally said, taking off Jessie's skirt; happy Jessie was so willing.

"James," was all Jessie could say as Sally sat behind her and rocked her in her arms.

"He fucked me and came in my panties, making me wear them here if I wanted to come tonight, he wanted people to know I was his," Jessie said as she began to cry. Sally was glad the room was pitch black, she wasn't sure Jessie would have been so honest if she had been looking directly at her. Sally kept rocking Jessie, feeling a tear fall on her arm she reached up and stroked Jessie's cheek.

"Are you his?" She asked seriously, hoping for an encouraging answer. Jessie shook her head, and Sally smiled victoriously as she enjoyed Jessie's head, making her tits bounce.

"Would you like to be mine? I would treat you a lot better than he would. I bet even if you say no, he keeps going. If you ever said no to me we would stop immediately, and we'd cuddle, and I'd kiss forehead until you feel better," Sally said, turning Jessie around and feeling for her hand. Sally placed Jessie's hands on her breasts.

"I've seen you staring at them baby girl," Sally revealed making Jessie gasp and blush.

"Would you like to taste them?" Sally asked.

"Um, I don't know, isn't that weird or like," Jessie tried to say as Sally pulled down the top of her dress and ran her nipple over Jessie's lips.

"Open your pretty mouth for Mommy Jessie," Sally lovingly ordered. As Jessie gasped, Sally pushed her nipple into her mouth.

"Suck it baby girl," Sally gently instructed, pulling Jessie onto her lap and began nursing her. Jessie sucked as she was ordered and quickly swallowed Sally's milk as her mouth was made full.

"Good girl Jessie. Be a good baby for Mommy," Sally cooed stroking Jessie's arm and patting her bare bottom while she nursed. Sally took a soft blanket which was folded next to her and wrapped Jessie in it feeling her skin becoming cool. Jessie snuggled into Sally, holding her full breast and making Sally's milk rush her mouth, softly cooing as she sucked.

"There's my good girl," Sally whispered bending down to kiss Jessie's forehead, enjoying the feeling of her breast being relieved of its heaviness.

Suddenly, Jessie remembered the time and pulled away from Sally, breaking their embrace.

"I have to go, James will be mad I'm so late," Jessie fearfully stated feeling around trying to find the exit. Sally put her breast back into her dress, only slightly annoyed the other one hadn't been milked as well and took Jessie's hand.

"Darling, you deserve better than him," she stated as she handed Jessie her skirt back.

"Will you be OK without panties? Those are too dirty baby," Sally asked lovingly.

"Yeah, it'll be fine," Jessie replied as she put her skirt back on. Sally led Jessie to the door, opening it and blinding both of them for a moment.

When Jessie's eyes adjusted, she turned around to find Sally standing in the doorway of the room, they just exited. She looked past Sally and saw what looked like a baby playroom. There were blocks and toys in a toy box, soft pillows, and blankets where they had been laying and a double size adult cot. Jessie turned to look at Sally, who smiled and closed the door behind her.

"What was that?" Jessie asked innocently.

"Mommy's playroom baby," Sally replied honestly.

"I saw um, diapers and stuff," Jessie said looked around the ground. Sally reached behind her and opened the door again.

"You would have, would you like a closer look?" She asked Jessie who began to blush. Jessie bit her lip, and her breathing became shallow as she just nodded.

"Say please baby," Sally coaxed, not wanting to push Jessie too far but wanting her to submit.

"Please Mommy, can I look at your things," Jessie replied, giving Sally more than she thought she'd get. Sally pushed the door open further, and Jessie walked past her, almost perplexed. Sally watched as she slowly made her way around the room, touching pillows and toys, running her fingers over a stack of diapers and looking at the collect of pacifiers.

"I use to love this book!" Jessie exclaimed. Sally smiled and walked over to where Jessie was standing.

"You probably still do," she replied, taking the book and reading the cover. Jessie looked at her waiting to see what she would do next.

"You use to love these too, and I bet just like this book you'd love them still," Sally said, picking up a diaper and raising an eyebrow at Jessie who just blushed.

"I don't know," she said, looking down to her feet, seeing her bare pussy remembering she wasn't wearing any panties.

"Well how about this, let Mommy diaper you, and then you can sit in my lap while I read you this story?" Sally questioned. She looked down at Jessie, who was shifting from one foot to the next nervously.

"We don't have to Jessie," Sally began to say before she was cut off.

"No. I mean, yes, I mean," Jessie stammered making Sally laugh.

"What do you mean little girl?" Sally chuckled.

"I want to try, I just haven't done this before," Jessie said, looking nervous.

"Then give Mommy your hand and come with me," Sally replied lovingly as she took Jessie back to the pile of blankets and pillows in the middle of the room.

"Lay down sweetie," Sally instructed as she gently lifted Jessie's hips and slid the diaper underneath her. Jessie played with Sally's hair as it tickled her face when she leaned across

Jessie and reached for the powder. Sally sprinkled the powder over Jessie who began to suck her thumb.

"Aren't you the sweetest," Sally exclaimed securing the diaper firmly around Jessie's waist. Sally sat back and patted her lap, and Jessie crawled to her and snuggled against Sally's ample chest as she began to read the story.

Jessie had almost fallen asleep when she jolted upright and looked at Sally fearfully.

"It's too late; I have to go," she said, reaching down pulling off her diaper. Sally tried not to get upset by the sudden change in dynamic and put the story to the side and handed Jessie her skirt. Jessie looked at her skirt and then looked down at the diaper she had almost taken off longingly.

"You said you had to go?" Sally reminded Jessie who looked up, clearly unsure of which she preferred.

"What should I tell him?" Jessie asked. Sally smiled, I told you-you needed Mommy little one, she thought to herself taking Jessie's hand and leading her to the front door.

"Tell him I kept you late because I needed help packing up and everyone else left before I had the chance to ask them," Sally suggested. Jessie smiled, she liked that Sally was true to her word, that if Jessie wanted to stop, things stopped. She liked that Sally didn't try to keep her or make her break up with James.

"Oh, I was thinking of telling him, that I'm leaving," Jessie replied with a cheeky smile. Sally gasp and wrapped her womanly arms around Jessie, almost smothering her in love and affection.

"But can you please come with me. I'm a bit scared," Jessie asked.

"Oh, of course, I am coming, Mommy is not letting you go near that monster without her," Sally stated protectively. Jessie lunged forward and kissed Sally on the mouth, taking her by surprise. She smiled into the kiss and wrapped her arms around Jessie once again breaking the kiss to look at her in her eyes.

"There will be rules with me baby girl, I'll give you all the loving you could ever need, but you've got to be a good baby for Mommy. I will give that little bottom of yours a spanking if you are naughty. Do you understand?" Sally explained sternly. Jessie nodded her head, which was followed very quickly by a, "Yes, Mommy."

Jessie nervously knocked on the door and was startled by its almost immediate opening.

"Where the fuck," James began to growl, stopping as he saw Sally. Sally saw Jessie change from her excited, bubbly playful little girl to an oppressed, neglected, and abused woman in an instant. She was happy she had come with Jessie, she needed her.

"Hi, I'm Sally. You must be James," she stated, reaching out to shake his hand. James reluctantly shook her hand but was still blocking the entrance.

"I'm leaving you," Jessie suddenly said in a whisper. James looked at her and then looked at Sally and back to Jessie.

"You're what?" He aggressively stated. Jessie reached for Sally's hand, who offered it to her instantly. She looked up at James, the man she had let use her for years and repeated what she had said, "I'm leaving you." James lunged for her, but Sally stepped in and pushed him back, making him fall on his arse. Jessie was surprised by Sally's strength and reached for her arms cuddling into them. Sally enveloped Jessie and turned her away from James so she couldn't look at him.

"Make a scene, and I'll call the cops," Sally stated plainly.

"You can fuck off while I get her things," she quickly added walking Jessie past him. She left Jessie in the hallway as she went back to James, who was still sitting dumbfounded on the floor. Sally grabbed him by the ear and threw him out of the house, shutting the door behind him. He thought about banging on the door but believe Sally when she had mentioned the police, so he just waited quietly outside.

"Come on, baby, show Mommy what's yours," Sally said, holding Jessie who had began to cry. Jessie walked into their bedroom and found her big travel bag. Sally went to the cupboard and took out Jessie's clothes and neatly folded them, placing them in the bag. They took her toiletries and laptop, books and the homewares she had bought. When they had collected everything of Jessie's, Sally turned around to find her standing naked behind her.

"You're going to need some clothes, little baby," Sally said admiring Jessie's lithe little body.

"I know Mommy, but I don't want to take these with me," Jessie replied, pulling on a pair of baggy jeans and a cropped top. Sally looked at the bed where Jessie had left her cum soaked panties and skirt in a pile on top of James pillow.

"Good girl," Sally said, walking over to kiss her forehead and take her hand.
James didn't say a word as Sally opened the door and led Jessie away from him.

"I was worried he'd start up," Jessie said sighing with relief as they hailed a taxi.

"No one messes with your Mommy," Sally whispered to Jessie before she gently pushed her into the taxi, happy to be taking her baby girl home safe and sound.

Roadside Baby

I saw her standing there on the side of the road looking lost. My truck is so high set that I quite literally saw her coming a mile away. She was standing there, kicking up the dust and playing with a stone, kicking it around in her pink high top sneakers. The road is a long and lonely place, and this particular strip is known for having working girls, but something about her made her look out of place. It was the way she didn't even bother looking at the trucks and cars that passed her, the way her denim overalls hung in an innocent way rather than a sluty one. As I drove closer to her, I saw she was holding a blue teddy bear by the ear, and I smiled at how pretty her blonde hair freely swaying in the hot breeze was.

"What are you doing here, baby?" I asked as I pulled up and pressed the window down. I must have startled her because she backed away but with nowhere to run on this barren, dusty stretch of road she didn't go too far. When she didn't reply, I opened my door and jumped down. She was surprised to see a woman driving that huge rig because her eyes sparkled in astonishment. She walked back over to where she had been previously standing and smiled down at her feet.

"I don't know," she replied softly. By the looks of her, she was no working girl. She couldn't have been older than 22 by the fullness of her skin and the lack of lines around her eyes. She looked me up and down, taking in my ripped denim offcuts and white trucker singlet under my opened red flannel shirt. I'd rolled the sleeves up revealing the bottom half of my two fully tattooed sleeves and work boots.

"So, you don't know why you're here? Are you lost? Are you waiting for someone?" I asked, taking a hair tie and tying up my long blonde hair in a loose ponytail. She turned to look up the never-ending stretch of road.

"I come from the town up there, but I'm never going back," she said, looking at me. I was at a loss as what to do. I knew what I wanted to do, but even though she held her teddy bear, I wasn't sure if it were something she'd want to do. I'll admit, I had made a couple of working girls my babies over the years on long nights when I was lonely. The easiest money they'd probably ever made, but I couldn't just pay this cutie to call me Mommy and then kick her back out onto the street. For one thing, she didn't belong there.

"Well, I'm headed down that way. I've got a 74-hour trip I'll be making if you want to come with me. No funny business I swear," I said, making her giggle.

"I don't have much money, but you can have what I've got if you take me," she replied. Oh, I wanted to take her more than she knew, take her out the back of my cab and rub my nipple over her pretty lips and feel her tonguing them as I rocked her. I composed myself long enough to reply promptly, stating, "No, you keep your money. I'm not about to take money from a baby." She laughed and thanked me as I helped her into my truck. I put her backpack with everything she owned in my cab and jumped into the front seat, turning up the song on the radio and pulled out back onto the road.

We had driven in silence for about half a mile before she spoke. She'd been looking out the window and taking glances at me. I pretended not to notice; I could tell she was worried I'd try something with her.

"I like your nails," she said softly. I looked at my newly French manicure and smiled.

"Thanks, baby. Maybe we can find a nice place to get yours done," I replied, making her sigh contently closing her eyes.

She hugged her teddy as the truck rolled on and was soon asleep. The rocking of the truck can do that to you, especially if you're not the one driving it. I pulled into a truck stop as the night began to get late and got out, making sure not to wake her. I'd learned her name was Becky and that she was 22. She was the youngest of 7, and her parents had been violent, abusive drunks. I'd found her after her father had kicked her out of the house because she wouldn't give him money to buy drugs. Meth was their new drug of choice.

I walked into the diner and ordered two steak sandwiches and two chocolate shakes, not the healthiest meal in the world, but it would have to do. I walked around the shop attached to it looking at postcards and other crap they sold while I waited for my order. Looking out at the dirty window back towards the truck, I thought about Becky in her cute outfit hugging her teddy as I felt my pussy begin to get wet. As my order was called, I shook off the feeling and went to pay. I had hardly taken two steps outside when I felt Becky's arms wrap around me in a tight embrace taking me by surprise.

"I thought you'd left me," she said almost in tears. I put the food down and hugged her back, involuntarily kissing the top of her head, relieved she didn't seem to mind.

"I just went to get some dinner baby. It's OK, Mel is here," I replied, soothing her. I could feel her heartbeat pounding fast in her chest as she pressed into me. It had taken all my strength to say Mel and not Mommy, and I was somewhat impressed that I had managed.

"Will you help me carry this back?" I asked her giving her a job to make her feel important. She nodded yes as I handed her the paper bag with our sandwiches.

"Good girl," I stated as she carried it back to the truck. We got back to the truck, and I put her back in the passenger seat while we ate. I buckled her in nice and tight and enjoyed her small tits bouncing as I pulled on the seat belt, making sure it was secure.

"Why are you a truck driver?" Becky asked as I handed her half of her sandwich. I half choked on my shake, laughing at her question.

"Because I wanted to be one?" I replied, unsure of what she was trying to say.

"Yeah but you're so pretty, and you have this whole cool, edgy, bad girl but nice thing going on. You could have worked in an office or something," Becky said, wiping her hands clean. I saw she missed a spot on one of her fingers and took a napkin in one hand and leaned forward to take her other hand in mine and began wiping her fingers clean as I replied.

"Becky, just because I'm pretty and edgy and cool or whatever else you think I am doesn't mean that I can't also be nice and caring. And as far as an office goes, I would hate that. I love the road I love the openness of it. I love that it let me meet you, for example," I answered honestly. I loved that she hadn't pulled away from me when I wiped her clean I think she liked being cared for.

"What do you like most about me, Mel?" Becky asked. Hearing her say my name made my stomach knot itself in delight. I knew what I wanted to say, that I loved that she was a baby who needed a strong, loving Mommy to take care of her, but I chose something more generic.

"You're lovely to be around, and you're not rude," I settled for. Becky wanted a better answer than that as she scoffed and rolled her eyes at my response.

"You could say that about a dog," she teased, making me laugh.

We finished our food, and I took her to the showers to get ready for bed. There was only one shower which worked, and I was surprised when she pulled me in with her and locked the door behind us.

"We are both girls," Becky giggled. As she began to take off her clothes, I tried so hard not to look at her young body. Sure she may have thought I was pretty, but my 38-year-old body looked not a day younger. She turned the water on, and it splashed on her perky tits making her small nipples hard as I passed her the body wash. I looked at her and knew I would have given anything to wash her pretty skinny body, feeling her pussy mound in my palm and rub shower gel over her back. When she realized I was still fully clothed, she giggled and began to help, me take off my clothes, which only made me raise my eyebrows.

"I'm helping," she said sweetly, and I let her look at my heavily tattooed body as I undressed.

"It's like a story," Becky said, paying attention to my chest tattoo. She gingerly ran her fingertips over arms, making me shiver, which made her very impressed with herself. She giggled and turned back to the water as I took off my pants and joined her. As we washed, she spun around playfully and stood facing me, her mouth and my nipples the same height. I had had my boobs done five years earlier, and their fullness looked beautiful so close to Becky's face. We showered in silence, except for Becky's playful giggles as she splashed in the water. By the time we got out, it was late, and I knew we needed to get to sleep if I was going to make the journey in time.

"But I'm not sleepy Mel," Becky playfully complained as I pushed her into my bed. She wore little short shorts that showed the start of her bottom and a singlet without a bra making her nipples hard and quickly visible. I had chosen my usual cotton knee length boxers and a baggy t-shirt, bed was meant to be comfortable.

"It doesn't matter if you're sleepy or not Becky, we are going to sleep now," I said with a slight seriousness to my voice she hadn't heard before. She quietened down and was asleep before me, which I found funny for a person who was not sleepy 10 minutes earlier. As she slept, I stroked her hair lovingly and gasped as I saw her begin to suck her thumb. It was all too much for me not to pull her close and kissed her forehead, making her smile in her sleep. I had thought about replacing her thumb with my nipple but chose to just hold her through the night.

I was just beginning to drift to sleep with the beautiful Becky in my arms when I woke to something wet and warm pressing against my leg. I yawned as I woke up to see Becky was also waking up, however far more terrified than I was.

"What is it, sweetie?" I asked, becoming concerned by the

look on her face. Becky didn't reply to me, she just bit her lip and began to shed silent tears I looked down to see she had slightly wet the bed. The front of her pajama shorts was soaked through, but luckily the thick 1000 thread count sheets had saved the mattress.

"Oh, baby. Did you have an accident?" I asked, rubbing her arm affectionately.

"I'm so sorry Mel I don't know what happened, you've been so nice to me, and I've just ruined everything. I'll go, you probably don't want to see me again," Becky said as she pulled away from me and stepped back.

"Stay right there," I said in the voice I would usually save for when a baby was naughty, but I wanted her attention.

"I'm not mad at all baby. I should have known, the teddy, the giggling. Why didn't you tell Mommy you were little and needed a diaper for bed?" I ask taking a gamble. *It can only go two ways;* I said to myself as I looked at Becky, who began to blush.

"I thought you'd think it was weird. You're so cool, I didn't want you to laugh at me," Becky said, looking at her toes which she was curling up.

"I don't think you're weird little girl; I think you just need a Mommy who will love you. Can I be your Mommy sweetheart?" I asked her as she looked up in delight.

"Oh, yes, please, Mommy!" Becky exclaimed jumping into

my lap now ruining my pajamas. I laughed and hugged her back, kissed her cheek, and began to strip the bed. I threw the sheets in the dumpster and took her hand, leading her to the showers once again. This time she waited for me to take off her clothes and I put them in a pile as my earlier fantasy played out. I took her in one arm and held her close to me as I washed her lithe little body. I rubbed her body until she was in a thick, soapy lather and then guided her under the water to rinse her off. I sat on the small ledge where we had placed our new pajamas and put her on my lap. She wrapped her arms around my neck as I spread her legs with mine and used the water as lube to play with her pussy. I could feel she was tight as I toyed with her pussy hole, pushing just the tip of my finger into her making her gasp and press her chest into mine.

"Don't forget to breathe baby girl, Mommy isn't going to hurt you," I coaxed reassuringly as I pushed my finger knuckle deep into her making her take it. I kept my finger in there as I rubbed her clit gently with my thumb and kissed her pretty lips. I loved that she had moaned as we kissed when I began pulling my finger out of her just to ram it back in, this time with more ease as she began to moisten. I caressed her arse cheek as she was gently finger fucked and held her as she came in my arms. Deciding she had had enough, I cleaned her once more and put on her pajamas. This time, I had chosen what she was going to wear. I had a stash of adult baby clothes and diapers in my cab for those times I wasn't interested in being denied, and I had chosen a blue singlet and a white diaper cover for Becky. I was grateful it was so late as I took her into the change room, and quickly diapered her. Seeing how cute she was diapered for me I had half a mind to make her go topless, but remembering there was a world outside of the doors, I held up her arms as I pulled on the singlet. Next, I pulled up the snuggling fitting diaper cover making her diaper press into her pussy. That's how I like my little ones, cunt dripping and begging to be fucked and having a diaper rub on your pussy all night will have that exact effect.

"Up you come," I said, picking her up and carrying her to the door. I quickly took Becky back to the cab of my truck and made her sit on the floor while I put on new sheets. I patted the bed and enjoyed watching her struggle to climb up into bed with her thick diaper and reached down to pull her up. She cuddled into me, and I patted her padded bottom until she fell asleep, contently in my arms as I pushed my nipple into her mouth and fell asleep to her nursing.

Becky became my trucking baby. I had a car seat made for her which could lock her hands by her side and her legs cuffed at the ankles for when I wanted unrestricted access to her. Those were some of my favorite times to fuck her. When she was diapered and held down, I would place a vibe in her diaper on her clit and reach my hand down her diaper to rub her pussy until she made my fingers wet with cum. I'd thread the chain of her nipple clamps through the finger hole of her pacifier and make her suck for hours which made her clamped nipples bounce with each suck and bump in the road keeping her horny. I kept her with me 24/7, looking after her and making sure she was entertained. I knew some of the other truckers liked kinky play, so I took her to their puppy play nights and got drunk with the puppy owners as I watched her play with their puppies. Life was grand. There was just one thing I hadn't got to do to her yet, and that was punished that cute little arse of hers. She'd been so obedient; she did exactly as I told, she let me fuck her when I wanted and how I wanted, she had let me exhibit her in her diaper to anyone I wished. What was also great was that she had happily traveled over the country with me. There was not a rule she had broken or a bratty remark she had said. But I still wanted her over my tattooed thighs until her bottom shone red. I had decided I would try and make her get in trouble. She knew she was not allowed to say no to me, saying red she knew was fine, but no was a different story altogether. I had decided to take her to a playgroup with other babies to see if I could trick her into saying no.

We approached the house where a Daddy Dom friend of mine was hosting a baby play day, and

Becky shifted nervously in her car seat.

"What if they don't like me, Mommy," she asked fearfully.

I looked at her and knew they would like her.

"Who are you worried won't like you baby girl? The other babies or their Mommy's and Daddy's?" I asked as I turned the engine off. I looked at her and waited while she thought about her response.

"Both. What if they think I'm not good enough or something?" Becky said, making me laugh.

"Oh baby, the will love you," I replied, opening the door and walking around to her side. My friend lived on a large property, so I had dressed Becky in a large diaper without a cover, happy I didn't have to conceal it. She had a pink dress with white teddy bears on the collar, and when she bent over even slightly, her big thick diaper was on full display. That's how I liked her on display.

"I'm so glad you could make it!" My friend Michael exclaimed, walking out the door and greeting me warmly. He bent down and looked at Becky in the eye, making her reach for my hand.

"Well aren't you just the dearest. You must be Becky, you can call me Sir," Michael stated, reaching out to pull the front of Becky's dress up. She squirmed and leaned back on me as Michael touched the front of her diaper.

"My little angel has this exact type on. I can tell you two will be friends," he stated, patting her pussy before turning around and walking inside. Becky tugged on my hand as Michael turned his back to us and whispered in my ear, "Mommy, do I let people touch me today?" God, she was such a good girl always wanting to do the things I wanted. I took her two hands in mine and kissed them.

"Yes baby, if a Mommy or Daddy wants to touch you through your diaper you let them today alright?" I asked her. I could tell she didn't want it; I hoped she would say no at some point today. We walked inside, and Becky was introduced to Angel, Michael's baby girl, and the two of them played with dolls in the living room as one after another more babies joined them. I got compliments at how well Becky played with others and how good she was. At one point a Mommy of a boy who was showing Becky dinosaurs came up and made her sit in her lap, and she did nothing to resist as the woman patted and rubbed her pussy while rocking her for an hour. As much as I was having a lovely time, nothing had made my heart sing as much as when I finally heard it. Becky had been drawing with Angel who had drawn over her picture. It was a picture of her holding hands with me. Becky had come up to me crying and showed me the drawing holding it up for me to see. Angel had then come over and told me what Becky had scrunched up her drawing, and a mortified Becky turned to me and when I began clarifying the situation she had interrupted me saying, "No!" I smiled and stopped talking, and Becky's eyes went wide with the understanding of what she had just done. She knew better than to interrupt me, and she also knew better than to contradict me.

"Game over little girl, come with me," I said as I took her wrist and led her to the couch. A few other Mommies joined us, and they watched as I pulled down the back of Becky's diaper and struck her for the first time. She yelped and began to cry as I slapped her arse time after time. I was telling her what she had done wrong and how disappointed I was in her. She begged me to stop telling me how she would be good again and not make the same mistake twice. As her bottom became a nice rosy red, I change from slapping her to spanking her. For me, the difference is in the intensity. A slap is a sting, a spank is a thud that sends something to a little's brain telling them to shut their mouths, and that's exactly what Becky did. She shut up and took her spanking until I felt her go limb in surrender to me. I rolled her over and looked into her eyes and knew she had reached her limit. Lovingly, I applied lotion to her arse and gave her her blankie from my bag. I lifted my t-shirt to let her nurse and kissed her forehead until her tears stopped flowing.

"You're lucky to have such a nice Mommy. When my little girl is bad, she gets a spanking and then sent straight to the corner," one woman said.

"You are such a softie on her Mel!" Michael said, bring me a beer. I knew I wasn't 'soft' on her; I just knew what her little limits where and when I'd pushed her far enough.

"When Angel is bad, she gets tied face down and fucked in

the arse while I spank her," he added I'm sure making Becky grateful she wasn't Angel. I smiled and stroked Becky's hair and patted her tummy.

"I don't need to do that to my good girl, she hardly does a thing wrong," I said looking down at her lips around my big nipple and her thumb gently rubbing her cheek with her blankie, full of pride Becky was mine.

New girl

"You can't live in there!" My sister exclaimed upon seeing the apartment I had just bought. Sure it wasn't in the most beautiful part of town, but it was no means unlivable. The building was 80's dated but fitted with the essential modern luxuries; the trump card was it was close to the cinema where I had recently been promoted to manager.

"It's pretty nice inside," I said, defending my new home. It was my first piece of real estate. No more renting and dealing with shitty landlords, no more having my food stolen by housemates, just my little haven from the world. She wouldn't understand. My sister Molly had married the rich boy in her high school class when they graduated college and never had worked a day in the career she studied four years for. She had become pregnant the day she graduated, and I'm pretty sure her husband had purposefully kept her that way for the last four years. But I didn't want to live like that. I wanted freedom, even if it meant having to struggle for a while and settle for something less than glamorous, at least it was mine. I continued to drive Molly home and helped her out of the car she was pregnant with baby number 5. I held her up as she made her way up the mansion steps and to the front door. Their maid opened the door for her and began gushing and fussing over her, so I said goodbye and walked back to my ten-year-old beat up car. It looked so out of place in contrast to this grand old family home with its perfect gardens and water features. *At least it's mine;* I said to myself driving away.

The cinema gig was fun. I got to eat all the popcorn I wanted and had tried every combination of soda you could think of. The other people who worked there and I made fun of the customers after the shift as we cleaned up and I had already busted three couples fucking during a screening. All in all, it was a lovely, routine, basic life. That was before I met Abby. She was the daughter of the owner of the cinema and had begun working with us because her father thought she needed to 'understand the principle of hard work.' When I had heard this, I rolled my eyes, but when I was then told I would be the one who would have to educate the princess in 'hard work' I lost it.

"I bet she's never worked a day in her life," I told one of my colleagues as we swept the floor. He wasn't listening, I could tell.

"I heard she's really hot, Bell," he replied, proving he wasn't listening to me. I just huffed and thought miserably about the next shift, which would be with her.

True to her word, she showed up on time the next day for her first shift. I was instantly annoyed with how beautiful she was. Her shoulder-length choppy cut blonde hair had its ends dyed pink, and she stared at me with the greenest eyes I had ever seen. It made me feel quite ordinary with my brown hair and brown eyes. She smiled sweetly when I asked her to restock the candy bars and count the straws. She didn't need to count the straws; I just thought it would be fun to make her. I showed her how to use the register and pour the soda so it wouldn't overflow. As the night progressed, I was even more annoyed by the fact that she wasn't a bitch. I had hoped she would be Daddy's little rich princess, but she was down to earth and didn't even hesitate when I told her to clean the restrooms.

"So how did I do?" She asked me while sitting on the counter while I swept under her feet. She had that flirtatious voice that had driven every guy she had spoken to mad with lust. At one point, I had to get a guy escorted out because he was holding up the line and became aggressive when I told him to leave. She was bad for business but stunning to watch.

"OK, I guess. I mean, it's only your first shift so I can't give you a verdict yet," I said as she jumped down and took the broom from me.

"I can do this for you, Bell," she said smoothly. Hearing her say my name made my heart flutter. *No, just fucking no*, I told myself knowing what that meant. There was no way I was going to be another one of those stupid people drooling over her. I handed her the broom and walked away, pretending that the posters needed straightening.

"You're like a grumpy Mommy, you know, Bell," I heard her shout. I'm glad it was just the two of us left, hearing her say Mommy made my cheeks blush.

"Well, there are things that need to be done and the longer it takes, the longer we have to work," I replied defensively making her giggle. I turned to see what she found so amusing putting my hands on my hips.

"I didn't say it was a bad thing," she replied.

"Look, Abby, just finish up there so we can leave," I answered, not amused by her games.

Our shifts continued with her teasing. She had called me this kind of Mommy and that kind of Mommy for weeks, and I had even realized I'd come to expect it from her, sad when she didn't call me a Mommy and wet with desire when she did. Hearing her call me that, and only me that made me wonder what kind of girl she was. I decided I had nothing to lose trying to find out.

The next shift, I did the usual clean up routine with her and waited patiently for her taunt.

"Gosh Bell, I can't believe you are such a bossy Mommy," Abby said without turning around to look at me. I was glad she didn't because she didn't see me open a lollipop and walk up behind her. I grabbed her arm, and she jumped, shocked to be handled so roughly. I pushed the candy into her mouth and held it there while I looked her dead in the eyes.

"Then do what I tell you to do, and I wouldn't have to be

so bossy, little girl," I assertively stated turning around and walking away again before she saw my face burn red. My mind was racing. I could not believe I had just done that; I could not believe my pussy was wet as I spoke to her like a naughty little girl. I hoped she would be cool with it, I mean, she had been calling me Mommy for weeks. As I was having a nervous breakdown, I felt a tugging on the hem of my shirt. I looked down to see Abby, sitting on the floor and looking up at me.

"I'm sorry, Mommy," she said, melting my heart with her big green eyes and candy red-stained lips. I didn't know what to do, but something came over me as I knelt and cupped her chin in my hand.

"Abby. When we are at work, Mommy needs you to be a good girl and tidy up fast. We don't want to be here all night, little girls like you need to be tucked up in bed, not walking the streets because you played too long after work," I found myself saying. This time I didn't blush, I practically swooned. This 19-year-old doll wanted me to be her Mommy. I a 27-year-old uni drop out who lived in an average part of town doing a less than average job for under minimum wage, I couldn't believe it. But I was sure as shit not going to pass up having a girl like Abby in my life. She nodded her head and put her lollipop back in her mouth, and I held out my hand and lifted her. We exchanged numbers, and as I walked to my car, Abby came running over and kissed me full on the lips.

"Night night Mommy," she said as the moonlight glimmered in her eyes.

"Sweet dreams little girl. Mommy will see you tomorrow," I replied, wanting more than anything for the next shift to start.

"Hello?" I said, answering the office phone. Abby was meant to be here twenty minutes ago, and I must admit I was worried.

"Mommy, it's me," Abby replied, she sounded scared.

"Where are you? Are you coming in tonight?" I asked her kindly sensing her distress.

"My car broke down, and I can't get there, I thought about walking, but it's so dark, and I'm scared. I didn't know who to call," Abby said in one breath.

"You didn't think to call your parents? Or a pickup truck?" I asked her wondering how many brain cells she had underdeveloped due to being babied her whole life.

"My parents are in France. No, I didn't think to ring a pickup truck, what if the guy is all touchy feely, I've seen movies, I know what they are like," Abby said trying to prove her knowledge.

"You know nothing little one. Message me your location, I'm coming to get you," I replied, making her whimper at my harsh comment. I felt my phone vibrate in my pocket, and I put her location in my GPS and told her to stay where she was. I told the staff they would have to work without me tonight, that I had to pick up Abby and the guys offered to come with.

"No, she doesn't like or want you. Stay," I instructed confidently as I walked out the door and towards my car.

As I drove to Abby's location, I wondered what I would do when I got there. Would I take her to work, would I ring the towing company to get her car, would I take her to my house? Maybe we would go to hers? As the thoughts ran through my mind, I saw her car on the side of the road. She was right; it was dark. I was hoping she would be in the car like I had told her and happily surprised when I saw her head turn around and be half blinded by my headlights, I got out of my car.

"Heard you need your Mommy little girl," I stated as I opened her door. Abby jumped out and flung her arms around my neck, making me stumble backward.

"I was so scared; anything could have happened," she hyperventilated.

"But nothing happened, and you're safe with Mommy, come on, come and sit in my car while we ring the tow company," I said reassuringly to her taking her hand and leading her to my car. I turned the heating on, she was clearly in shock from the one thousand percent non-scary event she had just experienced, to try and calm her while we waited for the tow truck.

"It's nice in here, Mommy," Abby cooed as she cuddled

with me on the back seat. I looked at my car and looked at her, confused.

"What do you find so deeply appealing about it baby girl?" I asked, brushing her hair out of her eyes.

"It has you," Abby quickly replied as if knowing the question I was going to ask. She began to stroke my stomach and slowly made her way up to my breasts, giggling as I looked down on her and saw her toying with my uniform buttons.

"Come here little one," I said lovingly as I moved her over my lap, so she was snuggling into my neck. I pulled her close and moved my arm under her and began rubbing her back with my hand as my other one unbuttoned my blouse.

"This is what you want, sweetie?" I asked in a soft low tone watching her nod in response. I pulled down my bra and let her see my breast as I took her hand and carefully placed it on the top of my tit, enjoying how she stroked it and pulled it out looking for my nipple.

"I would have never of guessed you would be so sweet little girl," I said in astonishment as she began to kiss and lick my nipple. I pressed her head against me as my other hand reached for the button on her short denim shorts. Unzipping them, I saw her cute pink checkered panties and stroked her over the top of them making her moan softly against my nipple. She stayed there, my sweet girl in my arms, her pussy being gently caressed. I slipped her shorts off her and rolled down her panties, happy she was so helpful. I was gentle with her as I spat in my hand and rubbed her already wet pussy with my palm, gliding my fingers down her slit and entered her without warning making her gasp and clench her pussy tight around my fingers.

"It's OK baby, let Mommy have you," I said as I began to finger fuck her softly. She nodded, and I felt her pussy slowly loosen, giving me unrestricted access. I wasn't interested in making her cum; tonight I just wanted to feel her. Feel her heart beat against mine, feel her wetness and her hot breath and tongue as she sucked on my nipples.

After a while I felt her go heavy in my arms as she drifted off to sleep and remembering the tow truck could be here any moment, I gently shook her awake.

"Baby, you can't fall asleep just yet," I whispered, making her stir. She opened her eyes just as the headlights of the truck came beaming around the corner. Glad I woke her in the nick of time I buttoned my blouse and got out to greet the trucker.

"You been here long?" He said as he hoisted the exotic car into the trailer.

"Long enough," I replied, smiling sweetly. I didn't want to get into a conversation with him. I wanted my baby back in my arms. As if reading my mind, Abby came and leaned into me, hugging me and turning away from the man. She dipped her head, and I felt her shallow breathing on my exposed chest just under my neck. The tow man noticed and tried hard not to look as I wrapped my arms around her making her feel safe and protected. I didn't care if he looked, but there was no way he would be touching her.

He secured her car in no time at all, and I told him the address where to drive it. He offered Abby a lift home but told him I would take her, and I was thankful when he left it at that and drove away.

"What a night," Abby said, walking back to my car. I unlocked it and buckled up her seat belt, kissing her cheek as I walked around to the driver's side. I turned the engine and began to drive to my place. I had decided on what she would be doing tonight.

"Are you taking me to your house, Mommy?" Abby asked as we passed the cinema.

"Yes, baby," I replied, placing a hand on her thigh and squeezing it slightly.

"I just have to stop into the store and pick up something first. You're going to wait in the car while I go. I know you'll be alright," I added, pulling up to the corner store. I got out, and Abby didn't say a word, she just watched as I left.

I had already ordered diapers online, but I hadn't bothered to order powder because I hadn't thought this would be happening for some time. I found the one I wanted and took it to the counter happy the woman didn't ask me any questions. I got back to the car and passed Abby the powder making her eyes go wide.

"All babies need their bottoms powdered before they get diapered," I explained to her which made her gasp and giggled nervously.

"I haven't ever gone that far before Mommy," Abby said, looking up at me nervously. I smiled at her; I couldn't figure out if I should tell her it would be my first time too or if I should act like I had a clue about what I was doing.

"It's going to be nice, Abby. Mommy is still learning, as well. If it's too much, we can stop baby. I'm not going to hurt you," I assured her as honestly as I wanted to about my skills. Seeming pleased with my response Abby turned the radio on and sang every song the rest of the car ride home.
I parked my car in the garage and took her hand, leading her to my door. I turned on the light and Abby walked in and looked at my things inquisitively. She walked to the window and looked out over the city.

"You have a nice view," she stated. I was somewhat aware she hadn't called me Mommy or used her cute baby voice, and I wondered if she was as nervous as I was.

"Is this alright, baby girl?" I asked her taking her to the living room and laying her down on my new black leather couch. It was cold on her thighs, and she squirmed around, lifting her legs off the material.

"Yes, Mommy," Abby replied. I smiled and told her that

we could stop at any time, that it wouldn't be fun for me if she wasn't having fun too. She jolted upright and wrapped her arms around my neck and whispered, "Thank you," in my ear, making me delighted she felt so comfortable and safe with me. I took off her shorts and panties quickly, making sure to put a blanket under her bottom so the cold wouldn't touch her. She lifted her bottom, and I playfully patted it as I placed the diaper underneath her and pressed on her hips to lower. I let her take in the sensation of the diaper before I opened the bottle of powder and sprinkled it over her making sure to use enough to stop any chaffing but not too much to make it messy. I fastened the diaper in place and looked down at her, surprised at how my life had changed in the last two months.

"Does it look, silly Mommy?" Abby asked, snapping me back into reality.

"No baby girl, you look adorable. Let me take off your big girl top and put you in something comfier though," I said, lifting her shirt off her and replacing it with a jungle themed long sleeve.

I took her into my bedroom, and we cuddled until we fell asleep, my last thought being, "She's not Daddy's little princess at all...she's Mommy's."

Naughty girls get spanked

There were two things in the world that I knew. One was that I loved learning how to make money, and the second was that I hated people. They just got in the way with their bullshit lives and lack of motivation to change their situation. That's why when I turned 21, the first thing I did was buy a block of land in the middle of the woods. I had gone to college the following year and let people use the land to keep their cattle while I studied, earned, and saved money. I thought it was a better idea than spending it on going out with people who couldn't go one sentence without mentioning the latest celebrity and their makeup line. So while they partied and vomited up their guts, I stayed in and worked on my primary skill online marketing. It didn't take too long before I was earning enough to pay off my student loans, and I began saving for the house I was going to build on my land.

Within four years, I had made my first million dollars, and I took half and had my dream home built on the huge acreage. I maintained my online marketing business and comfortably worked from home for the next three years. Life was great. I no longer had to deal with the outside world and their bullshit. However, I was lonely. There wasn't anyone particularly interesting in the one shopping strip town I lived in, and I didn't want to be down there enough to be considered a local. So I decided to advertise for a house cleaner. I thought if I'm going to have to be around someone they might as well be doing something to help me.

I had to wait six months before I met her. Lana. The woman who swore to me she was American but her very clear Russian accent made me wonder. It honestly didn't bother me though because she had my place looking divine.

"You need to tidy these things," Lana said, moving my washing out of the way. I looked over my computer to see her folding the clean laundry I had sitting on a chair for the last three days. She had a point, so I just smiled and looked back at my computer.

"Did you hear me?" Lana said in an angry tone. I shut my computer lid down and looked at her shocked she would speak to me like this.

"You work for me Lana, not the other way around," I said, getting up and knocking the neatly folded laundry to the ground and walking back to my computer. Before I reached my chair, she grabbed me by the arm and was pulling me back to the front of my desk. She bent me down and kept me pinned by her forearm and spanked me hard for the first time.

"You naughty girl. Making naughty things. When I clean you not make mess," she said as she spanked me over my jeans. I struggled to break free, but she just kept spanking me until I gave up. I thought it would be over then, but she turned me around to face her, undid my zipper, pulling my jeans down roughly making me sway forward and back. Turning me back around, she pushed me over my desk and spanked me again, and this time I felt it. She took my panties in her hand and pulled them up into my arsehole and spanked my arse until I could feel its warmth, making my face burn red.

"You not make mess now yes," Lana said, turning me around and sitting me on the desk making me look at her. I had never been so embarrassed. In my whole life, I had never had someone spank me or pull my panties the way she did. What was worse was that I could feel that my panties were not only in my arse but that they were wet. I had enjoyed this. I nodded to Lana, who just huffed and walked out of the room. Something came over me, and I quickly dropped to the floor and began tidying up the mess I had made. The marketing adds I was working on could wait; I didn't want Lana to be even madder at me.

The memory of Lana spanking my arse stayed with me for days. Probably because the sting that now greeted me every time I went to sit lasted for days. I had slept on my stomach for the following few days and had made sure that the house was tidy when Lana was due to work the following week.

As she walked around my house, I followed, showing her the things she didn't need to clean rather than showing her what she needed to clean. I couldn't tell if she was impressed or not. Her deadpan face made me nervous as she went from room to room and inspected it.

"You learn lesson fast," Lana said, making me filled with pride. More pride than I wished it had as I blushed bright red and looked at my toes when she turned and saw.

"You like?" She asked. I wasn't sure what she meant so I looked up, still blushing.

"I like what?" I asked in the politest tone I had. She gestured a spanking, and I flinched, making her laugh.

"Good girls need no spank," Lana explained, taking my hand and leading me to my bedroom. I had assumed I'd forgotten to clean something or put something away when she pushed me on the bed and had half accepted that a spanking would occur. But I was surprised and very wrong when I turned around to see her standing at the edge of the bed with a toy cat. I frowned slightly unsure of what was going to happen when Lana climbed up onto my bed and pulled me into her arms. I let her, remembering how strong she was and how much I didn't want to be spanked. She pushed the toy into my arms and took each of my hands and made me hold it.

"Play," Lana ordered. I looked down at the toy and wondered what she meant. It wasn't an instrument, and I hadn't played with toys since I was a kid.

"Don't be bad girl, I say play," Lana said, repeating herself. I took the cat and moved its paws along the bed, hoping this would satisfy her. Luckily it did, and she left the room, leaving me confused and unsure of what was happening. As I got up to follow her out of the room, she came back through the door and snapped her fingers in my face.

"No. Bad girl. Lana say play, and Katie play," she said, making me jump back on the bed and play with the toy cat. I looked at it and had to admit it was cute. It was brown with a white tummy and green eyes and a long soft tail. I played, and Lana watched until she reached into her bag. She pulled out a magazine and sat on the end of my bed while I played with the cat, snapping her fingers when I stopped.

Eventually, Lana finished her magazine and reached her hand out to me. I had assumed she wanted the cat back, but I had grown somewhat attached to it, and I shook my head and held the cat to my chest and away from her.

"Katie now Lana no wait give kitty," she said in a warning tone I didn't want to test. She took the cat and smiled at my disheartened pout as I flopped my hand in my lap dramatically.

"See you ncxt week little baby," Lana said as she left the room making my heart skip a beat.

What does she mean little baby? I asked myself for the next five days. It wasn't like I acted like a baby. I didn't even have a baby voice. I was serious and studious and interested in math. I was puzzled and confused and annoyingly turned on, remembering Lana's sexy voice and words.

I tidied the house like I had the previous week and followed Lana around as she inspected my efforts again.

"Good," she stated as she took out the toy cat and pushed it into my hands. I excitedly cuddled it involuntarily making her laugh and me blush when I had realized what I had done.

"Do Lana's sweet girl like kitty?" She asked, patting my bottom over my skirt. I nodded and looked into her grey eyes. Something about them looked different today. Upon closer inspection, she looked different today. Her usual jeans and sweater combination was replaced with a low cut halter dress that came to her knees and heel sandals she had taken off at the door. Her cleavage, usually hidden away, showed just how full and round her breasts were and she wore natural-looking makeup, making her look sophisticated and mature. Catching me staring at her, she laughed.

"What you look like?" Lana said, taking my hand and leading me into my bedroom once again. She pushed me on the bed like the previous week and came to sit next to me straight away. She pulled me onto her lap, and I sat, my back to her between her thighs as her large breasts pushed into my neck and cheek. She turned my head, making me look at her, which brought my mouth to her nipple.

"So you like na?" Lana asked, pushing her tits into my face. I pulled away from her and caught my breath. I had never been so close to a woman before. I had never been so close to anybody before. Lana shook her head and pushed my face back between her huge soft jugs and pushed them against my face. They were soft and smelt like her perfume. I stopped holding onto the toy cat and lifted my hands nervously, wanting to touch her. Sensing my nervousness Lana took each of my hands in hers and placed them on her tits. She showed me how she wanted to be caressed, saying, "Like this," as she lifted them and let the weight fall. When she took her hands away and let me do it by myself, she said, "Yes good. Like this," and closed her eyes, making me proud I could please her. She let me play with her for a while before she took my hands and turned me back around, so I was facing away from her. She held me in one arm as her other hand reached under my skirt and patted my legs apart.

"Yes, good girl," she said as I pushed out my pussy to meet her fingers as she began to run her fingernails over my panties, parting my pussy lips and pulling on them gently.

"Off," Lana stated, pulling at my panties. She took her hands away, and I wriggled my panties off from under my skirt.

"And this," Lana added, pulling my shirt up and over my head. I held the top of my skirt in my hands and looked at her expectantly.

"I didn't said skirt. Do I?" Lana asked, making me worried I'd be spanked. I shook my head and turned back around as she pulled me back onto her. She lifted my skirt, grabbing a bunch of it in her hand and stuck her two fingers in my mouth with the other.

"Suck," she commanded sternly. I sucked immediately until she was satisfied, gagging multiple times as she shoved her fingers deeper down my throat, saying, "Take it. Take it," over and over in her warning voice. She pulled them out covered in my spit and pushed them straight into my pussy, forcing herself in making me yelp.

"Hush now," she ordered as she roughly fucked my pussy.

"I've never," I said breathlessly, desperate to let her know I was a virgin. She raised an eyebrow and slowed her onslaught enough for me to begin to breath normally again.

"New?" Lana asked as I teared up. She bent her head and kissed my cheek as a tear fell on it.

"New," I replied. In an instant, I saw a gentler, kinder side to her. I guess she no longer saw me like a naughty girl who needed to be fucked into submission. I learned what her replacement was though pretty quick.

"You are baby. My baby. I look for you," Lana said with determination. She stopped fucking my pussy and moved from behind me and jumped off the bed, leaving the room. She came back a moment later with her bag. She took out a pacifier and a bib. Sticking the pacifier in my mouth, she rubbed my cheek with her thumb, looking into my eyes lovingly. She kissed the tip of my nose and put the bib around my neck. She unzipped my skirt and pulled it down quickly. Taking out a pull up with unicorns on it, she pulled it over my legs and patted my bottom once it was on.

"Cute," Lana said as she picked up the toy cat and took my hand and led me back to the couch.

"On my lap," she said, pulling me to her. She cuddled me close and put the toy cat who I had taken to calling kitty on my chest and began to speak.

"You my baby now," she said as she patted my thigh. I had moments where I felt like an adult in baby gear, but I had longer moments where I felt totally at ease dressed in what she had me dressed in. I couldn't understand it. I decided I didn't care and began to play with kitty as she spoke.

"You call me, Mommy. No Lana no more understand?" She explained. I nodded again, attempting to take out the pacifier but she put two fingers on it and pushed it back into my mouth.

"Baby do what Mommy says. When baby bad, Mommy spank, when baby good, Mommy love, OK?" She continued. I liked that Lana was so clear about what was going to happen.

"Baby work sometimes Mommy work sometime. Most of time, Mommy will give baby toy and tell her wait for Mommy come back." Lana said. She had thought this through. I spoke through my pacifier, "Mommy. I don't have to work too much; everything I do is passive. I earn money while I sleep." Lana's looked at me confused, so I wriggled out of her embrace and walked over to my computer to show her. I sat in her lap and explained to her how my business worked, how I had employees, and where she could see the money coming in.

"You are clever baby. I no take your money baby. I just want you. Mommy still work, but maybe not so much," Lana said, patting my head.

"Come, little girl, Mommy want to watch you play," Lana said, putting my laptop on the couch and taking me back to my room.

Who is Tina Moore?

Tina Moore has enjoyed the lifestyle of a Mommy Domme for several years. She began exploring kink and BDSM in her youth and found her love of being a strict Mommy Domme in early 2000. Tina Moore is now an author of many MDLG and ABDL themed novels.

Having enjoyed many years in the kink community, Tina Moore combines these experiences with the sweet and naughty things her baby girl does to bring you tantalizing and salacious stories.

Follow her on:

Author Page on Amazon

Instagram @tinamoore.kdp